Hôtel Amour

Hôtel Amour

Deryn Rees-Jones

Seren is the book imprint of
Poetry Wales Press Ltd.
Suite 6, 4 Derwen Road, Bridgend,
Wales, CF31 1LH

www.serenbooks.com
Follow us on social media @SerenBooks

The right of Deryn Rees-Jones to be identified as
the author of this work has been asserted in accordance
with the Copyright, Designs and Patents Act, 1988.

ISBN: 978-1-78172-784-3

A CIP record for this title is available from the British Library.

The publisher acknowledges the financial assistance
of the Books Council of Wales.

EU GPSR Authorised Representative
Logos Europe, 9 rue Nicolas Poussin, 17000,
La Rochelle, France
E-mail: Contact@logoseurope.eu

Cover photograph by Fidan Nazimqizi

Printed in Bembo by 4Edge ltd, Hockley.

... and the words give out their scent, and ripple like leaves, and chequer us with light and shadow....

— *Virginia Woolf*

It was time

THE HOTEL

The hotel, which had once been one of the most famous brothels in Paris,
occupied a discrete section of the quiet street. Here, if you listened,

you could hear the world in the quality of its movements. You could hear
the loops and unravellings of the particular, coming together and then,
washing away.

Here,
every wobble of the world in the moments of its creation, paused,
and for a moment, she thought, here the sky had managed to

place itself, unknowingly, on a great hinge of between-ness: here was space,
time, and, if you, too, paused to look up, here dreaming, here thinking,
you could hear the clouds flirting

across the late summer sky; here you could see, later or earlier, say, the
smear of

colour as pinks and oranges bled evening to night, night to dawn,
here, &

L I S T E N!

In the nearby cafés, the rustle of pages turning in books and newspapers
had become amplified, even the wingflaps of birds,

of eyelids opening and closing at the start

& end of the day, telescoped their sounds into new meaning.

(Words lifted themselves into the air as if they, too, were
                birds   wings   leaf   flutterings.)

SSSSSSSHHHHHHHHHHHH

The sign outside the hotel, up in the 9th, was made from pink neon.

In the boldest letters it spelled out

AMOUR

She had booked the room the previous week,
    imagining how it would feel at that pinprick moment
    in the future

when the afternoon darkened, and she found herself

sitting beside the window, watching the sign bleed its pink light into
the room.

AMOUR

Bleedspill, fluorescent. Here. Elsewhere. Perhaps a little hum. She liked
to imagine —

she liked to imagine the couples who had been there before her, the
temporary residents, ghosting and overwriting themselves in

captions of feeling: the tenderness, the

moments of indulgence, joy, boredom, vulnerability.

Here, too, was a history: of sabotage,

harm, violence, fear, all working its way into the fabric of the building, gnawing, biting, sucking, swallowing, settling and edging in, at the door, the window. . . .

Desire.

She flicked at the thought — stretchy, powdery, twitching — alive between her fingers.

She thought — imagining that moment now —

of the time in the Orangerie, when she had stood admiring a picture she
knew very well, but which was new to her friend, who stood beside her.
In it, everything was precise: the women were tending to a man who sat
inert on the counterpane. There was a jug in the foreground. The detail at
the back of the image on the painted wardrobe was a picture within a
picture. It

reminded her of all that had happened. The ravaging, ugly, ordinary,
a-synchronicity of illness and of death.

And yet, as the friend pointed out, with great deliberation,
the perspective had been put into the frame all wrong. As space got
unravelled, as the family unravelled, shook themselves into their feelings,
actions,

so time

shuddered & realigned & shocked.

Narratives, promising all, like lives, snapped off without reason: bud, blossom, branch, were cut down suddenly

(with a pang she remembered the old tree in the garden, how it had fallen in what seemed like slow motion, its roots exposed & naked like a huge —

and now she saw it — a huge lung, upturned before her like a ripped-out diagram from a medical textbook).

When she imagined the room in the hotel, it was like this:

it gave her a way of keeping something locked tightly in her mind: a projection of something that had been/not been,

endlessly creating itself

in an imagined future. There, too, everything was not quite in the right place. A mouth

pressed into a shoulder saying quietly, yes, like this, like this?

A hand shifted, weight shifted, cells moved from one body to another.

It was a kind of voyeurism: the spooling out of the strange pattern of two bodies interlinking, a rhythm, a cry

and all the pauses of display and revelation, the realignments of fluids and breath, the animal noises; a glance, a movement of something that was happening.

It was a dreamed space. It was a poem. And, there she was, standing in the crux of a future time, taking the key from the concierge, placing it carefully in the old-fashioned keyhole, pushing open the door. Yes.

The virus had blurred her vision, it had made her see things askew or even sometimes in double.

Fragments continued to assemble themselves.

She had read, somewhere, of a condition, Paris Syndrome, where visitors came face to face with their fantasy of the city and, disillusioned, became dizzy, or hallucinated, vomited, fell to the floor with rapid heart rates. It was a kind of culture shock.

She imagined it was happening even now as all along the Rue de l' Hôtel de Ville the sirens from the red and yellow ambulances of the sapeur-pompiers streamed and curled like long blue ribbons.

At night, in her own rented apartment in Saint-Paul, the river traffic lit up her room. She slept with the blinds of the huge windows open, the Panthéon a pale ghost at her feet, and the cranes that flanked the ruined shape of Notre-Dame lifting little blinks of shadow and light into the sky.

There was an order to each morning. Below her, a man camped in a tent beside the road, made coffee on his gas burner, did stretches and press ups, as she herself made coffee and watched the city make its daily commute: bicycles, cars, rollerblades, scooters, everyone's wheels moving faster and faster to their destinations.

Écoute écoute

Coucou coucou

From her window she could also see a Dutch barge, named *Bâteau Ivre*, moored up on the quayside on the opposite bank of the river. A poem in the flesh! Behind, in frame,

was Notre-Dame. Up near St Sulpice, Rimbaud's poem, 'The Drunken Boat', was written carefully out, she knew, in precise stanzas on a wall.

Words. Pictures. Things.

Now, more than ever, it was easy for her to get lost in the squares and winding streets of the Marais.

And it was tempting, always, to stitch everything together, to make meanings from it all as on the world went, with its particularities and rhythms.

This morning, a serious young priest, in his long, black cassock, played ping-pong patiently with a group of young boys.

Écoute!

Coucou!

Like a lyrebird.

How easily everything suggested itself to her, pinning her to meaning; everything happening in the instant recalled itself via memory. Someone had sprayed in neon, cursive pink

Féminins don't stop fight nearly the victory

across a stretch of the closed-up booths belonging to the bouquinistes. She wondered, really, what it meant, and let it irritate her, the way it called out for a line break.

Old films

spoke to and through her. But

who was speaking the voice-over to her own
$$\text{small life?}$$

In Bastille, the angel at the top of the Colonne Juillet towered over the traffic, his golden wings outstretched.

The summer, too, stretched lazily out, but soon

the leaves from the plane trees would kick at her feet. *Leaves. Lines. Rhymes.*

Napoléon, so the story went, had wanted,
instead of the angel,

a huge bronze elephant.

In Victor Hugo's *Les Misérables* the elephant — at that time still only a plaster mock-up that slowly disintegrated and which was populated by rats

— becomes the refuge for a small boy. Now only the stump

of the elephant, her plinth, remained.

Monuments. Wars. All that had been laid waste, the emptied spaces, shook with their harms.

One night, she dreamt of lightning, and a huge shadow-scar in the shape of a tree that marked and blistered her body as it struck.

One morning, she had been well enough to take a longer walk.

For a while she sat in the Place des Vosges as some students were rehearsing scenes from a play. After a while, she realised it was *A Midsummer Night's Dream*, the part where Bottom wakes and realises he has the head of an ass and Titania wakes and sees him.

Quel est l'ange qui m'éveille de mon lit de fleurs? The young girl, as she spoke, gave him a look of displeasure as he met her gaze.

To see Bottom, transformed with his huge donkey head, was indeed marvellous. And how it reminded her of the madness of love when one wakes to see

the ordinariness of the lover transformed.
Such cruel

magic.

The children had no ears for their donkey: instead, the young boy wore a pair of headphones.

Beside her, a woman was picking up the mess of her dog. *Zéro! Zéro!* she called to his pale eyes and big, wolf-like features.

Somewhere in the hotel — *amour amour* — an Englishwoman, she had been told, was writing postcards to strangers as part of some clever, autofictional project.

Life went on.

Some afternoons, she surfed the net, aware that she was looking for something she could not find. On the pages for the Lost Property office, amongst the keys and notebooks and musical instruments, someone had posted up a picture of a kitten

LOST   FOUND

The kitten had no logical home, and so it sat there, in both sections, waiting for someone to decide where it belonged.

Le pinson, le moineau, et l'alouette,
Le gris coucou avec son plain-chant....

The French rolled over her, half-understood, half-recognised. Zéro. Coucou. Now life was like this, she thought. A body remembered itself in fragments. Books, fluttering pages talked to each other, sometimes with a kind of fury, sometimes with a kind of tenderness. Paths and splinters, ways forward, false starts, and steps, meaning making itself in a prism of reference. She thought about the woman in the hotel, sending postcards to strangers. She imagined a girl making a path through long grasses that over time would become a path. She thought about the small helpless creature, sitting in its virtual state of displacement, perhaps now with a home, perhaps not, no longer a kitten, but a cat.

Look. Glances at meaning, at thought. One. Two. She blew into her palms to warm them as if they were a small instrument.

Suddenly a lime green bike propped up beside the métro sign was nothing short of beautiful.

She shook her head as if resetting a watch.

One afternoon she took the métro to Pigalle to meet a friend.

The sex shops, peep shows, strip joints, sat side by side with the local pharmacy, and the covid testing tent. A glare of green and yellow neon.

That day,

the rain had held off. And she had walked aimlessly with the other tourists in the cemetery. Dark and cool, it would soon fill up with heathers and chrysanthemums for All Souls.

The sun hung low. Before she made her way back home she saw two little girls playing by the métro vent, cheerfully daring each other to throw empty paper coffee cups into the air.

She watched the small vessels rise and rise,
as the subterranean heat blew up into the boulevards.

The red windmill

in Place Blanche stood poised behind them,

and the girls' thick hair streamed skywards, as they laughed, as if they, too, might become untethered from the earth

and, light as paper themselves,

float up.

Often, she sat in the muteness of her own

limitation. Sometimes, she spoke hesitantly with the vocabulary of a five-year-old.

She took photographs —

of squares rewilded, full of dusty sparrows and overblown flowers; orange dahlias, lavender, yarrow.

She took photographs of memorial plaques, remembering children lost or deported to the camps.

One day, as she turned a corner, she was met with the sight of the school children in the Rue des Rosiers, lined up with their gourds to celebrate sukkot, the harvest festival.

She took selfies as she sat alone in cafés, and at night,

sometimes, the river traffic, that slid past the Quai des Célestins, noisy at 3AM, would wake her. The strings of lightbulbs looping beside the river bars, twinkled like a necklace made from childhood teeth.

On rainy afternoons she watched old films in the order of their chron-ology — *Paris qui Dort, Hôtel du Nord, Les Enfants du Paradis, Les Portes de la Nuit, Love in the Afternoon*. Then the city would remember itself in black & white where it would linger, without colour, in stilled frames in her head.

Atmosphère! Atmosphère!

La vie est belle

I love the way it all hangs together

Once, as she watched the screen in the corner of her room, she glanced up and was startled to laughter when she saw a grand piano dangling in the sky on a wire as its owners tried to remove it from their fifth-floor apartment.

Once

she woke to see the moon so big and close it seemed to want to leave the sky and

lodge inside the window.

She caught her breath. She touched her face.

She had pulled herself back from something, she knew.

Now a sense of herself quivered & puckered like the damaged edges of a
piece of cloth

that brought to mind — like suddenly falling through the trap door in a
stage set — a half-formed,

half-coherent memory of standing in her grandmother's small back kitchen.
She must have been three or four. An old wax spill, used to light the stove,
had been left carelessly on the windowsill, and the flame had caught the
edges of the curtains. She stood, tilting her chin, looking up at the column
of flames as they swiftly took hold of the gaudy 1950s cotton print. There's
a fire, she had called out,
            but none of the adults in the next room had believed her.

Shapes and feelings remembered themselves to her as part of her childhood,
igniting like small fires all through and across her skin. The sounds drifting
from the old telephone exchange at the top of the hill, its click-click-click,
which echoed inside her; the monkey-puzzle

tree outside the old sailors' rest home; the evening walks along the back of
the quarry; and the water tower, a huge sandstone oblong, like a turret in a
fairy tale

which she looked out to from her bedroom. Now new shapes and sounds
overwrote

themselves.

Blood,

coppery,
that she might have mistaken for dirt, smeared her underwear.

She could feel in that instant, the metallic taste in her mouth, the small gap
where a milk tooth had been.

And with a leap, all things sat alongside, beside

themselves once more, realigning the glances of colour and sound being
drawn from the canvas:

Angel Delight, Prawn Marie Rose,
a drowned ship, the chestnut-brown sandals
with their worn innersole,
their cut-out leather uppers
like arches for stained glass,
the nylon zipper on her A-line skirt,
the brushed pink cotton
of her sheets,
the snake charmer

who had nodded and smiled at her,
the tooth-puller, in his tent, surrounded by
monkeys in acrobat costumes tethered
to each other in the old square
in Marrakech, the call
to prayer from the minaret,
rose petals in the water fountains,
nettlebeds beside the stream
in Eglwysbach, the milk churn
at the hill-top, the soft, oozy wander
of a cow herd at dawn and dusk,
the rich smell of their hardening pats
in the grass; lamb's wool adrift on the grass like
fallen & forgotten clouds and the
spooled cassettes in her bedside drawer,
out of which came low, sweet throbs
of song; her grandmother showing her
how they taped the windows
in the war to stop the shattering glass.
Sideboards, soda siphons, antimacassars;
a woman in her silver-
spangled two-piece, at the circus
on the trapeze, above the safety net;
her mother brushing her dark hair
then dressing her beside the radiator
every morning; the red scooter which had become,
as she rode it round and round in circles,
a horse, on which she balanced,
its harness bright with silver,
as it tossed and shook its invisible
jangling head,
the bit tight in its mouth.

Her own history sat documented in fragments, completely adrift. And each day, the métro at Pont Marie held itself up to her like a dance card. Then the coloured lines & numbers tangled themselves into an impossible knot of threads. She felt herself continuously strange.

In a nearby courtyard, someone had set up a citadel of

bird boxes and beside it, hanging from invisible threads, was a flock of tiny origami birds. They bobbed and nodded to each other in the breeze. The little bookshop before the square had a window that

opened on to a wall of symmetrical books like a

swan's wing. And always the sirens on the Rue de L'Hotel de Ville.

For weeks, now, the courtyard she passed through as she entered or left the building, had rung with the flattened notes of a young boy singing scales. The opera singer on the third floor had started to rehearse her students from her living room.

Above her, on a lower floor, a pianist was practising, over and over, Chopin preludes.

The singer's voice and the piano notes darted together and became entangled in incongruous accompaniment. She enjoyed the stops and starts and

hesitations
& repetitions

as the pianist returned, over and over, to the difficult bars.

The old psychoanalyst in the ground floor rooms paced between appointments in the tiny tree-filled space.

Somewhere everything rhymed.

And when she tried to, to wrench into shape the sounds and pictures, the poems sat like little squares, or monuments to thought,

held together like a concertina

into which she wanted the world's air to breathe.

(Later, so much later, though, and she did not know this now, they had checked out of the hotel, and sat for a while together beside the Seine, she and X, or Y, quietly in the afternoon sunshine.

As much as she remembered, she invented him, algebraic.

Above them, in the near distance, was a pompier on the rooftop in his red jumper with its curved trim, and royal blue line.

Look! X had exclaimed, or she had exclaimed. Or perhaps she had simply looked up and seen —

Around them sirens and traffic and river noise. And all her forming and reforming memories, of hospitals, & hotels, & hostels, all the counted-out occasions of loss, of death, edged in.

She had told him about the dog, Zéro, and he'd said, bursting into the laughter which was his beautiful hallmark,

Imagine, two dogs, though! I'd call them Being and Nothingness.

She smiled, and thought about Rousseau and Voltaire, Sartre and de Beauvoir, self and other, left and right, Laurel and Hardy, Ginger and Fred,

up and down, old and young, poetry and prose, X and Y, love and hate, life and death.

She thought about their children and their unchildren. She thought about his losses and her losses and how the air between them ionized and electrons jumped across the space between him and her. She thought about love and time.

It was hard letting go. Somewhere, the two dogs that sat in their mind's eye together, nuzzled and sniffed at each other. She took a breath and he took a breath and somewhere

out across the rooftops, song and breath and air mingled and dispersed.

Then, *It's time*, she'd said.

She was imagining and remembering and let things morph and settle. It was weight and weightlessness. It was bodies, and chemicals and histories and speeds and textures and glow.

And now they realised that light was falling. In the plane trees baby bats swooped and flickered. They walked, her hand in his coat pocket, the way they'd always done, and let their pace adjust to each other. They didn't talk now, but knew the direction they would go.

After a while they settled beside the Pont Neuf. He was as old then as the day they had met. He was twenty, in his old blue sweater, and as time peeled away from him, so it surged into her, and her hair was stained with grey and her face wore itself differently.

Then,
as if the hem of her dress, or the corner of his jacket
had caught on the pink-orange glow that spilled from the sun setting,
everything suddenly lit

and blurred

the fractures and burrs and swells and joys and terrors of their parallel lives spilled and rose and what their bodies had stood for started to flare and burn until flames ran and roared and suddenly — yes —

she called out

but they were gone

as the day was gone,
without alibi, or futurity,

except in their own slow past.

Above the bridge where they had sat together, the sun dropped. The pompier, in the distance, was so small now that it seemed like he would fit in a pocket or a hand.

He looked out across the rooftops of Paris.

And darkness fell —

doucement doucement —

as he carefully finished his cigarette....)

But back in the Rue des Martyrs, near the hotel, it was still late morning as the day beckoned her. The smell of warm pastry and sugar seeped from the glass-fronted stores that lined the street. The chefs, in their long white caps, impassive, staring out of the floor-length windows in one of the bakeries, whisked the egg-whites up into great flumes of white, into domes that stiffened in quiet emulation of the Sacré Coeur, which

came in and out of view as she crossed the street.

With a sudden blast of feeling, she remembered the roses, sent to her all those years ago, at the end. She remembered how slowly the flowers had blackened at the bedside, took on a scorched feeling, and how her hands had snagged on the thorns when, at last, she made herself throw them away. There had been a moment, too full, too strange, too familiar,

& then that moment had become something neither of them could quite hold.

Edges, loss. It was over and it was beginning. A memory held inside her of his body, the sweat on his skin a glistening skin of silver, a forcefield of beading fire. It made it impossible to touch him without him also slipping

away. Outside (she was elsewhere now again) the cool, spring wash of sky was papered over by apple blossom, translucent, drifting from the trees.

And there she was now in a future where her temperature rose and the sheets were soaked and cold. Outside was filled with the sound of helicopters. Her own breath was echoey and falling out of her as she tried to make some use of it. She lay face down and arched her back to open up her lungs as if to tempt air in through her mouth, its broken 0.

She wondered if her shoulder blades might shoot out quills and clouds and air and dust and feathers.

Now, as she walked, surreal flights of language flew across the air in envelopes of untranslation so that her mind struggled to unstick the flaps at their edges.

She listened. She paused, wanting nothing less than a knife to slice deep into the heart of them.

When she'd left, the water was in short supply; it was dirty and needed to be boiled. There was endless summer rain. The prices of fruit and vegetables in the supermarkets had soared. Blocks of cheese and litres of milk and pieces of fat-ridden meat were padlocked to shelves. Now a country lobbed up drones and another shot them down before they touched the earth like some awful, gone-wrong game of tennis. Small children were being starved; women had been raped, hospitals bombed. Death was everywhere. Cruelty was everywhere. There were narratives of pain seeping into the earth. She moved her gaze from screens to newspapers to the grand palaces of law and justice that sat derelict and abandoned.

And and and

but but but ....

But where did a person reside? (And there a part of her, a small, fleshly, sore part of her, might have answered, between the living and the dead, as she looked for the door key, and lifted it slightly so as to turn the heavy, metal lock).

In her apartment, she opened the blinds. She put the apples she had bought into a bowl on the kitchen table, snipped off the stem-ends and thorns from the unscented yellow roses she had bought in the Friday market. With a look, impossible to read, she placed them in a vase on the windowsill next to the little trail of carved, hardwood elephants with their ivory tusks.

Linked, trunk to tail,

they followed in a fixed chain of arrested movement. She

saw them but no longer saw them. To whom had they — like thoughts, like feelings — once belonged? They reminded her of the elephant enclosure she had visited each winter, with friends, in the cold, bare, inland landscape of west Wales. She would dream of the elephant, but, like Schrödinger's cat, she had never seen her.

As she moved about the room her thoughts wandered again.

The inked scribbles on the sheaf of typed pages, still sitting in the corner of her work desk, looked archaeological already. The pills she now took, not yet decanted from their packets and boxes, reminded her, as in her imagination she arranged them, of a string of rosary beads. Like her writing, they had started to feel like another way of both counting and avoiding time.

Each room in the hotel was different, the concierge had told her. On the walls were prints of women, naked, rounded and smiling, their breasts painted high on their torsos, the pink of the areola spreading like a circle of eyelashes, and their limbs draped with impossible lengths of material.

The colours were soft and brought to mind, in a sudden upsurge of sadness, Piero della Francesca's great nativity. Transposed to a fifteenth-century Tuscan landscape, Mary stared down at Jesus who gazed up, arms outstretched, on his blue baby mat, which was, in fact, the draped mantel that hovered, mysteriously, around his mother. The ground was like the ground of another planet, with its scorched brown foliage. It was hard to work out Mary's expression. And Joseph, who was sitting behind her, one leg crossed, the sole of his foot bare, was somehow too intimate with the gaze in which she held him. His face seemed unfinished, his eyes closed.

The singing angels watched on; the 'o' hole of their guitars open like the perfect o of their mouths, or the word joy itself.

It was not joy in Mary's face, she thought.

Here was a world

unfinished, without shadows. What changes and what renovations could be made?

A magpie perched on the makeshift barn that framed the couple so that sorrow sat watching over them, la plume de ma tante, a feather in a hat.

For a year she had been so unwell she could not leave her bed. Later, as she began to walk again, she remained insular, as if behind glass. This retreat from everything had, at first, not been a choice. Now, it seemed as if this sense of herself in recovery was so estranged, so dismantled, that eros

errors

fractures, terror, the endless uncertainty, the precarity always

that sat alongside the story she told about herself or others told about her

could not coalesce or heal.

(Somewhere, her daughter was sitting at a desk in another country, looking out at a garden, lifting her eyes from a screen, or a page.)

(Somewhere, her son was stretching his long arms, shaking from them the deep wet silks of brightly painted wings.)

Then the letter had come, forwarded from her old address.

The anticipation of meeting turned inside her like some endlessly-turning piece of perfectly-made and intricate machinery.

This was a life —

plans, distractions, interruptions, moments of recognition. A shape, if ever there had been a shape other than the immediate one, laid itself out to her for a moment,

and in her, too, like birds arrowing, making marks in the sky.

The letter smelt of nothing except itself. There was no hint of the breath or skin of its sender. Inside, the loops and curls of handwriting made their own picture on the oblong of folded white paper.

At seven, she went into the bathroom.

Beneath her clothes, her body was its own continent, full of the geography of the many pasts it held, which vibrated between her and all that was around her. She shifted as she looked at herself

in the mirror, and then shifted the mirror. She held herself in front of time like a cartographer might hold a slew of land in the square of its frame. Bodies rose and fell and grew in her and the world fractallized from and out of her and all her harms and sweetness. She was faceless now in the mirror and without her lower limbs. A scar sliced her abdomen from one side to another. Another scar, that traced a similar line, but which had been scripted with a steadier hand, overlaid it. Vein, scratch mark, stretch mark, blood blister, age spot, freckle. She moved her gaze about herself. Clavicle. Breasts. Ribs. Mons veneris. She squatted down and the mirror caught her new shape. The fold of her belly unfurled into the folded envelope scar of her umbilicus as she looked down. The lives of others knotted & held inside and across her. Little fires of memory sprang up. Fireflies flew from her like notes of song. She was precarious, actorly, unmothered, untethered. She pushed fire and love and fierceness around her body. She paused and unfurled herself again. The soft fur at the top of her thighs grew wings and flew and hovered. She mapped herself again against light and shadow. She watched her body hold and catch and move with her breath. The square of the mirror held only this much of her; and then her gaze shifted again

as the early evening light from the street shimmered through the window in a sudden stream, showing her to herself anew, and leaving its shadows and dapples across her like a bright shifting screen of pixels or cells. She was nothing and everything and forest and water and cloud drift or sound. She took a breath. She was savanna . . . dust . . . pollen. . . .

All around her, Paris glimmered and wobbled in its own light and auras. Later, when her taxi drew up at the hotel, the street was otherwise in darkness. The neon of the hotel sign continued to raise a cluster of sensations in her she couldn't quite place.

Amour, like a murmur. Amouramourarmouramouramourarmourar-mouramouramouramour.

She nodded to the woman at the hotel desk who, smiling, handed her the key, and wished her a pleasant evening.

The room's lights had been left on, and it was softly glowing. It made her want to somehow join the light; to strike matches, light candles.

There was a faint smell of something memorable, that seemed to translate itself from the pink haze of the sign

and sink into her skin. After a few seconds she put a name to it. Of course. Somehow, there was a story still to be told.

She had waited. And a force inside her trembled & rose

like a past that kept on happening, that had already
become the future, but from which she was already walking,
(she knew now)

walking away.

She opened the window, took off her shoes, began to undress, and very
slowly placed her watch on the waiting bedside table.

(i)

On the blue sofa in the Rue de Navarin there's sunshine, a ghost
of summer. The Eiffel Tower, like a woman, brazen, each night
unravels, slips out, over and over, from her glittering dress. I kick
dead leaves and rhymes along the river's lines. The digital world
continues its insistent & galaxial glow. Then episodes of happiness
break through. Our small, impossible lives bow, nod, yawn,
stretch out. I'm thinking about the lovers, smoking, now, beside

the voiceless river. There's grief in everything, and suddenly you.
As bedfellows, I think, we're filled with terror. But I like the way words
stray to you, your finger light against my nipple. I like the way the o
leans tight into the e in cœur. How does it end? My thoughts bed down,
tuck in, wild as a pathogen. Error after error. *Sshhhhhh.* Who's that
in the mirror? But look. Our bodies know us and are less than neat.
And I'm here, whatever that means, and alive, which at this point seems
quite a feat.

(ii)

Check in/check out. Here's a note on the English edition.
'We touch each other. How?' Yet more quotation. But couplets
are not mine, nor songs. I need elaboration. A flood of selves
moves out across a memory. Poetological. What do we know?
The hotel corridors are tight and long; the metal keys
are heavy in my dress. *Hôtel Amour.* And the cabbie laughed.
Rue des Martyrs. J'y vais. Je suis là. So, your French is good?

Hipsters and coffee in the heat. The fan is wooden, 30s, colonial,
the courtyard airy; the bath like a pit of pink and black,
seams in the marble. A bed in which to drown. Conscience,
forethought. Another kind of play. But actually, my French
is bad. Before desire, retreat. Before you, my own cruelty. But I wasn't
cruel, I was sad. You of the world and sometimes not, the lost and
lively ghost that you've become stands in again, again, again for what?

(iii)

The hotel corridor is psychedelic; the carpet, with a sense
of humour, wears navy & pink, a pattern of phalluses,
Ganesha with his raised trunk and gentle, resting head.
Outside, on the pavement, I see from my window, a slab
of what, steak? A pound of flesh, pulled from
a restaurant crate? Starlings peck, pull at their find.
A car revs in a distant street. Ghost heart, lost breath.

A hundred ways of loving and a hundred harms. You push
at the self, but we can't be translated. Who's good at forgiveness?
Severance? Loss. Memo from me: hell, like love, can be
climbed out of. Now I want nothing but you to stride in
through the half-open door and to be not that puddle
of sinew & blood on the floor, but a poem, alive again.
You, holding me, in ordinary arms, like air.

(iv)

When you were gone, I suffered most from homesickness.
But it's a hard art, a retrospective, and an old story, us
on the page, alert to each other, distracted. There was always
a language between us, even apart. When you whispered all night
Come to me, I came. Conspirateurs, just setting forth, and candles lit
in the lost chapels of our hearts. Now I see you, weepy,
in your blue pyjamas – even as we perch on the cliff face

of our plenitude, where, like some cartoon angel, *LIFE!*
threw back its shoulders and you kept on walking down the
staircase straight towards me. Who knows, I thought, as I
stepped out, brushed a face, rude, against evening skies, but
kept on coming (more fool me) & even now
calling out to you, when who knows where in the mobius
strip of us we've landed.

(v)

There's lots I'd like to clear up here. Clear out. Not quite
like a letter, with its awful clutter, which I owe you, I guess,
even ten years later saying *Well, we did the right thing by
doing nothing, rather wildly.* Cherophobia's a thing. And perhaps I
owe you nothing. A thought which keeps coming back to me
like a hurricane out of season, which is where the world
is now; which sort of hits the spot. Life is messy. You knew

that better. You were a dark lake that I fell into. I think I
was in shock. I think what happened was a diversion. Anyway,
I felt it. Fell apart. Quietly, drove myself into the ground. And
in the garden dogwood bloomed in spring, then rose
to flaming scarlet in the autumn. Sparklers in a car park.
And the sun still rising. Fires
from time to time still burning. Who'd warrant it.

(vi)

At Christmas you'd do magic tricks, light up the papers
from the amaretti, so they'd drift, a flock of burning angels, cupids
little loves, in air. Words. Enough to set a house on fire.
And now a thousand yous in ash, in words, in flames, settle
in a sudden burst of light/now snow, my books laid out
across the floor in which I see your hand, your eyes, your hair.
Why do I reach for this? Perpetuating what? Perhaps I'll find

in Paris squares where lime trees and their scent bring tenderness
and heat to cells, a joy that's mine. Rest with 'the spider and the
gentle bee.' There's dust, letters, dead leaves already on the
Quai des Célestins. Mid-summer and the war still rages.
Another child goes missing. Somewhere a family counts its
terrors. What to do. What to do with the shock, mess of
what came before, après-coup.

(vii)

Dearest. Hello. It's us, again, late for ourselves, out of step
but alive and singing, this imaginary cantata. I'm planning, later,
to assume a cool English brilliance and meet you slender
in a slender shade beside the gardens on the other side of town.
Starry night, starry stars, lemon in the soda. Tee-total, and my face
a picture. But that's so far from me that all I hear from you
is laughter. And love, like the cost-of-living life is surely

astronomical. So I'd be Elisabeth. Or Sarah. There's no risk of
disclosure, except of my own self which honestly baffles me, there
on the open page. Move on, let go, the self-help chatter, echoey, dull.
Now I dream of a landscape, of not being the city, in siege. You're the horse.
Like the shriek of a chorus: Calibri, Garamond, Times New Roman,
Baskerville Old Face, American Typewriter. *Applause, applause.*
Barbie or Oppenheimer. These days, we're all so split.

(viii)

What was it to love? And then to love again? Dopamine and dis-
orientation, the propaganda of romance springing like a white hart
from a brook in resistance to the mind's rules, time's box,
and somewhere, yes, catastrophe. Desire, dizziness, making
the body fall outside of itself. For it was falling, and us
like Roadrunner and Coyote, the roof of the high building never-
ending as we sped across clouds and then disbelief, un-

suspended, scrambled to find the undrawn ledge. Descent.
Drives. Madness of a sort. And a ghost like a doppelgänger. My
head pressed to a cool wall. I remember it, now, the pain of you
not being there at a party, a glass of champagne like a bouquet thrown
by the bride, then the walk home, solitary: the snow,
and the house, quiet in the lowlight. The *mweep mweep*
of the silence. Me in a nightie like a wedding dress.

(ix)

When I was sick, I'd conjure you: shapeshifter, chimaera,
vital, inevitable, you as you always were, wrapped in a shield
of smoke and mirrors. In your soldier's coat, with that
boyish expression, shy as doe, bright as button, you were
stuck on me, we were stuck to each other. But I should
have known, and in some ways I did, how the pain
of papercuts is always delayed. Could we be different?

There were scenes. I like the expression. But there's more.
In the room of us we were childlike, loving, addicted as a bomb
to its own ticks ticking. We had come to an end before
we began. And those moments of calm were the simple drug
of joy: us tucked in a hillside tent, a small bird, unnamed
in a hedgerow — fledgling firecrest, wheatear, wren —
joining us there, without permission.

(x)

Who wants to know about the bodies of the lovers?
In sex, the best is metaphorical: love does that, moving the material
to spirit, one foot off the floor, impatient, jiggling, *whaaaahoo*, and
almost transcendental. Then sooner, or later, love gives you
the slip, slips you out of time and space, and unwarranted in a
memory holds you. You could spy on the you of it, or I,
drunken, romantic, with that scotch on ice,

could observe the merge of genitals, skin, bringing
everyone in, now glorious, now silly. Such a crowd, so
untethered, as particles, flecks, lives, move and flow.
But your eyes, for example, which haunt me still,
speak history with their hurt kindness, their
imagination's stealth and scheme. How it lingers
in my body: pain like a meme, an undertow.

(xi)

I've got used to death. Age does this: piles up the bodies so that,
given half a chance, post their hard exit, they bow, pirouette, form
an orderly queue, as if patiently waiting for bread, or the groom,
with confetti at a wedding. Once, a friend said yes, you've lost
a whole village — poetic licence on her part, excessive. But I started
running my eyes across maps, small, distant places. X marks the spot.
The gone, with their bags and collapsibles, coats, birdcages, letters,

epiphanies, really are gone. And I'd like to say that there was
HAPPINESS (yes caps lock), even as I stood up from the old sofa
to say good night / goodbye, knocked a wine glass from the table, fell
asleep mid-movie, even in the long nights — distant, feverish, calling out,
ridiculous — when you'd left / not left me. Always, like a barb
in my ankle, it lodges there, you: a feather-stab of bracken,
something just found.

(xii)

Strange for a muse to be such a dab hand, a whizz. Forever
making plans, and cooking supper. Now I'm in my own high room
undreaming and undreamt beside the rain-streamed windows.
Is it the violence of the nothing now that I can't keep inside,
as the body starts its mendings? Lost breath, failing cells.
A hundred ways of loving and a hundred harms. Somewhere, you sit
blameless in a room, the light on your face reinvented, soft; and me

like a kite flown from the beach as you look up to hold me, catch
the wind, a thread that pulls like time against the landscape or the shore.
We didn't sleep much on those stolen nights together: fevered, tethered,
waiting for breakfast, toast and eggs, under silver salvers, with our
plastic swipes and luggage. Like morse code, you're a pulse, even now,
dash then dot. We live in the gaps. I like the way after all this time
-.....-.. --- ...- . -.. / --- -.. / .-.. --- ... - it's the heartache not the
heart that stops.

(xiii)

What's this, then, the poem as confessional? I don't think so. Or
machinery to clean the wound. No, it's not that either. If it's
a box, it's quiet and three — no — four dimensional. Outside,
there's a violence lurking that's not mine, seeping from my phone
into my hand. Perhaps it's inside too: lives breaking, a bad movie.
A stick of dynamite in an old back pocket. No superheroes and no
script. Meanwhile, the hotel fan is a blur, a whir,

a strange propellor. I take a bath, the windows open. I've spent
a long time putting a body into words. Autopoeisis. What is it
now, as it stretches out? Scars, marks, the skin's frailties, pores,
movements, a shifting set of cells? Excitotoxicity? My toes
turn on the tap. I'm trapped in a gif of my own making as
the lonely world startles, shudders, coughs in the
early hours. . . . then silence,   & we are adrift.

(xiv)

What does love fight for? The push and pull, the ordinary high
and squalor? Love's coincidence / invention brings bodies for a time
together. To earn our place, in the new life, fleshly, unlonely,
something gets carried across on our wings of desire, and away.
Now abbreviations (abs) are sweet as kisses. X X X
on a day where texts and objects touch and shimmer.
Take all my love, you gentle thief. AWAY. Love taps

into the angels' song: whispers in the library or the burnt-out
stadium. Entanglements and new beginnings move us, too, are
ink, song, splits, spilt on the page. Listen, as I lay there mottled,
on the operating table, my heart on the sonogram was clearly not
broken. Cardiopoetic, *padam-padam*, a fist making all things move.
It's not a squirrel, I can confirm, not a forest walk, a naked swim,
a late-night drive. It's an ampersand, a bear in a cave, dear creature,
                                                    a plum.

(xv)

On my slow walks there were fields and puddles, corncockle,
foxglove, dandelion and thistle. I shake out the ordinary
like the pink ribs of an eiderdown, lie down with you there
as an old woman tends a grave in memory, unknot your
words from my mouth. To rid you of me was combustion, an
engine fired, or the little light flick Zippo, turning one thing to another,
or on. Oh, I'm so sensible, so full of measure. I don't

like the thought of a toxic emission in all that fire. And, anyway
who says to a lover, I've a stone to get carved, without feeling
the bother, or like you've stepped in, somehow, to a gothic novel.
I don't think you minded. You were kind. But I minded,
could not quite attend. Two magpies strut beneath a lime.
I tune in to life like a maestro with her tuning fork,
step into my body to let slip   all that is not mine.

(xvi)

Darling, what night did we not sleep through storms together,
when thunder was like bins, rolled out by kindly neighbours,
mundane debris of the world on forecourts, in turn put out
by our un-misery? Eros. Roses. Roars. As lightning forked
and shimmered, as we stood under its bright chancery,
my chin edged to your shoulder, finger looped in your cool finger,
separate, still, by the blinded window. Look, the great elm, the cherry!

In the mind's eye we are alive, still, blasted like blossom, aching,
spidered into ribs in fractured glass. And what night did language
not stop us, send us to each other's arms, even at a distance, even apart?
Think again of that thunder, that breaking sky. Think of a number,
a psalm, a future, a quiet place. Pick a card, any card. Accept
the unyielding way the world has of offering us each other.
Think of us, that last time, lost to each other's disgrace.

(xvii)

Over and over like an analysis. What I like best in a poet
or rather the poem, by which I mean — of course — the
poet, is an ability to lose the self. You, over and over,
neither one thing nor another, a voice working, seeding
speeding, settling and unsettling, playing through, not even
an imagined world or other but the chords, let's say, of the self
elsewhere. So here we are, like an orchestration, with no orchestra,

no self without an other, others. Perverse, perhaps, illegible.
Aaaaaaagh. That's the part of me I miss. Me doing unspeakable things
beside the blue-green river. You, doing unspeakable things with
me beside the glassy river; and I like, for now, that they're
unspoken, never the same. There. Not there. Over and over.
And now I've somehow, how I don't know — paralysis
of missing selves, cells, in the torn world — fallen for, and into
this & lost myself in losing you.

(xviii)

Back in the imperfect world, I've minutes before a train.
There's a man throwing up outside a boarded-up window. There's
a burst of light that warms my shoulder. There's pavement glass,
there's your hand on my shoulder, there's me turning round,
with tears in my eyes, the old car, familiar, and me no older.
There's a car smashed outside my door, we don't know the owner.
There's your hand, tanned, on my knee as we drive, the satnav

and our favourite songs, played over and over. There's tea
in a flask, there's the smell of grass as the sun drops, the simple
warmth of my head against your chest, your mouth and mine; and us
as a thing. What a funny old creature. There's the furious guy
in the street below, bashing each day, the parking meter. Across
the world there's a hummingbird somewhere at the nectar,
almost weightless beside a tree.

(xix)

'The poem is lonely.' The poet, meanwhile, dreaming, wakes, mutters
turns pages over in sleep. Now nights are lit by our trails. Moths flutter.
We eat cold rice by the light of the fridge. Mouth-to-mouth.
Cold wine. Love pools; at 3AM water simmers on the gas flame.
When we talk, blossoms rain down, snow falls, like we're locked
behind glass. In a globe, at the bedside, the little plastic splinters
respond to violence, gently. I do not know how your hands can hold

so much sorrow. I do not know how a body can hold so much.
Lightning whips the distant hills, pressing the window, the skyline,
neither inside nor out. The room illuminates, the night burns up.
Can the close world hold us? Wars hang from the walls like maps
made of tissue paper. Sellotape and small tears peeling. History
rises. Here is the spill of blood in damp earth. They are all now.
The night of the riots, my father's gun like death, again, tucked
                                                    beneath the bed.

(xx)

'Do I dream you, or you me — / in essence, a dry cough
of a question.' Lungs falter. The hotel sleeps. The virus,
I think, still has us in its grip. The air is cool on our
cooling cheeks. Memories erase. Night times, I listen for sirens,
stuffing their ears against the dreams of the living. Exhaustion
makes the soft pillow a stone. One hundred years have passed
and someone, in error, knocks down your door. The lift

like a coffin, rides the floors. And I remember, once, how
a woman walked past me in the orange light of seaside arcades,
her collar up and her eyes burnt low. She might have been all
that madness makes us. Rage rages. Poems, like spectres, hang
in the air. You send back my love, in a little box, to pierce
my heart like a lightning flash. Do I dream you, or you me?
I sing her song. Her song, her roar, her shaven head.

(xxi)

The summer makes no argument against us. The legislators sit
beneath the trees. So here we are in separate solitudes of making do,
making the measure of ourselves beneath the spotlight. The square bed,
slow with nothing but a white sheet, slowly, like a zen miracle.
And not even the smell of soap powder to drown the senses
in soft cotton. We would use ourselves up in a bed like that,
the two of us: smudges, marks, on a tautened canvas.

When a wren bursts out in bright falsetto; when a dream catches
in my wrist like water; when winds rub against old harp strings; when
July's rains like us, this, are endless, continuous, keeping us, soothing us;
at what moment does the word break? Or love. At what moment
does the world spring, to remind us, this hour, that is not our own?
At what moment is everything over? The noisy blackbird at the gatepost,
warns us: as night falls again on love, damage & all our private parts.

(xxii)

Is it always midnight in these poems? Or the year's midnight,
Lucy's Day, when, in the black Citröen, we'd set out
one afternoon. We were fresh at the start of things, untouched
by the you or I of it, 'things that were not'. You'd kissed me
against the rough fir in the forest, the fir, which is the poplar,
the great elm, the linden, ash, oak, the apple tree one particular
summer, which was when we were driving west. Time passes. Then,

in the dusk, we were heading for home and from nowhere,
three girls weighted in white dresses, their yellow hair crowned
in foliage and burning candles, burning walked towards us. Turn back,
you'd said when we'd past, and in the end, we did, and the long bare
roads were empty but for our headlights. They were gone, as when next
you, with your usual courtesies, were also gone, and the dark
dropped as I drove, with only the bristling forest at our backs.

(xxiii)

What is love then but unlearning, the shivers, tremors, small specks
we are, shifting on the shifting stage. What is love in the new place
where age leaves us like a hat, say, forgotten on a bench, its owner
leaving cells, debris, scents, heat in the summer's breath — oh —
straw or linen, an old form, fluttering then singing like leaves
in the memory space: imagination, desecration, all haze. What is love
in the face of trial & pleasure, in the broken world we'd like to live in

fixed-fixing, breaking open, opening and writing over in
-to new ways, in a new rhythm? I think of you and the empty page,
walk my fingers across your landscaped face. How tender this is
and the strange mirror that our love was and the error
never ending. Laughter brings us for a moment together.
Then we begin again, on & on, run into something —
elsewhere, and the past lets go of itself, at last, is strange.

(xxiv)

The world has shrunk, steps back in time. A blackbird
sings its old desires in a thought I've conjured like a picture book.
And thoughts now snag themselves like water at the edges
of a glass. At night the radio becomes an 'inland murmur', as if
quotation might remind us how to be ourselves in sleep; we're not.
Then sunrise, breakfasts, turned down sheets, the lift falling
like a dumb waiter as we hold ourselves to the border

of nothing — the perfect burning summer where lines and lives break
to desire, imagination, which has no time or object. O.
Time to leave the old hotel — though, of course, in a way
you'd left already. The possible opens like a blue sky, blue-dark
and shattered with starlight. The fizz of light: sparklers in
a hotel car park. Our lives apart become the memory
of a memory, thought before the thought.

(A bee sleeps in a flower.

A thought rests

in the canoe of its own making. A stag beetle

hugs a blade of meadowgrass. A tree sinks roots

into purple soil. A frown unfolds from the furrow of its making. A star

wanders to the night's embrace. Starlight

spins rapidly across magnetic fields.

A fly suspends itself in amber. Then a pause unravels.

.

So I dream in the space between your breaths,

my hand across you I'm a rowboat, oars loosely tethered, at the pier.

So I sleep,

after a sweet song,

casein and whey,

baby at the breast.)

THE GARDEN

All summer, the tiny sash window that looked out over the garden, had been jammed open. The cord had bounced off its spool. Now the joiner had come to realign the weights. There was much talk of pulleys and runners, and the need to ensure that the new nylon cords did not fray.

She was wary of the joiner and his desire to talk. He carried his tool kit up the stairs and indeed, she thought, as she followed him, and noted the edges of his jacket were slightly frayed, that he had the air of a doctor attending a dying person. They both wore masks and kept a safe distance. Together they carried the distance as a child might an overfull glass of water.

He told her he had been sick with the virus as she,

too, was sick, still. She said nothing,

but the whole house remembered — the heart pain, like something the size of a cathedral had collapsed inside her — how she could not breathe. Once, in the middle of it all she

hallucinated the ceiling was falling in: a little edge of brown rippling. And then space collapsed in on her.

She remembered how once, in the night, on one of her visits to A&E (always there was neon-red light, always, always the half-light, dusk or dawn, *courage courage*, like an installation) the doctor   wearing her hazmat suit

touched her wrist, looking for a pulse. Her heart. Her heart. Was it still even there?

Or had she dreamt this. The slow distracted walk round the hospital. The buttons in the lift counting themselves, backwards, the tiny valve revolving on the mask, which she found she was wearing, like the head of some origami elephant,

tuning her in to what?

One weight would be switched for another slimmer one, said the joiner, turning towards her, fussing at the dog, and letting her lick him.

And all the time he dealt with this, she thought, this work of balance, fixing, weighing of the souls. How did it all cohere? The now slipped into history.

The bed was not quite a square. The sheets were white and her body also white, mottled and stained and losing all definition as it sat in its state of disease, her lungs calling for each next breath. Steady now, there now, like a pillow pressed over her face. History

flickered in her hands as her phone threw images at her and all she could do was sit late in the night and watch, as if her illness was the only way her body could hold the horror. There in the warm, safe house.

It was strange, truly strange, she thought, to have the little broken window
— which had meant some nights a gale

blew into the bedroom preventing her from sleeping — fixed. It had
meant that every day flurries of autumn

leaves swirled in the corner of the room
however many times she collected them on her hands and knees.

As she knelt, she would hum that sad old tune to herself.

And, although it was late autumn, the petals from the buddleia continued
to bloom and fall, little purple dots becoming little brown dots, and still the
blackbird and the goldfinches flitted on and out of all the green .... all the
wild things that had seeded and reseeded. . . .

and earlier than ever, now, were nudging up from the soil, or from the
edges of the stick-like branches, green shoots.

When had she heard it sung last? Yves Montand singing and making it ache
like age itself.

Yves Montand who had died, after the final shoot, of a heart attack, in a film about a man who dies of a heart attack.

Yves Montand who had been married to Simone Signoret. Who had had an affair with Marilyn Monroe on the set of *Let's Make Love*.

In which Bing Crosby and Gene Kelly play themselves,

singing and dancing a little.

Art. Life. She pictured herself in a high, large-windowed room. How a mind drifted off.

Time shook the seasons and something like a snow globe on freeze-frame halted and refused to recalibrate.

The world had taken on an apocalyptic feel. And yet, she called to it, to words, in the only way she knew how: to beauty, to history, to

a future she couldn't quite call optimism, couldn't quite call hope.

Everything was changed — intensities forced up on some invisible dial of pain. War, floods, the virus, the burning world and all its realignments.

She must learn to inhabit it — the world — as she learnt once more to inhabit herself.

I / we / he / she / they / you / I / we

(Somewhere, her daughter was sitting at a desk in another country, looking out at a garden, lifting her eyes from a screen, or a page.

Somewhere, her son was stretching his long arms, shaking from them the deep wet silks of brightly-painted wings.)

Do not look back.

(But where was there to look

when the shops were boarded up and the streets empty and everyone was locked in their houses and everything

just as they had been warned it would, began to happen; it made no sense not to remember, the lists of names of the dead.)

The joiner told stories as he worked away at the window and seemed to want her there — he told her about the ways you could fix a window,

as he petted and played with the dog who had no

intention of leaving either of them alone. Perhaps he was lonely. Perhaps he recognised in her a part of his loneliness. Perhaps, in an

uncomplicated way, it was one soul saying to another, Here I am, and this is my life. Here is a part of me in stories. She listened. Everywhere there were stories; sometimes stories she could hear and sometimes stories she could fall into. Yet words held her back.

It was infuriating, and fascinating and diverting and yes, just then a moment of intimacy and

connection almost boiled to its abstraction. She felt

herself yet not herself. She was, she realised, impatient, but somehow enthralled. It was hard to turn away. One moment, she said, checking her phone, and nodding,

leaving the joiner as he removed the whole window

like an eye being lifted out of a socket

with all its cords and tendrils and nerves.

Always

there were messages.

Buy this, love this, reply to this, do this. She had needed to leave, to step out of that delicate web of intimacy the joiner was spinning around them.

One moment.

And to do this, she stepped into spectatorship of the fragmented world again, where votes were being counted, where settlements were being bombed and burned, where cites were being razed, and violence bled from everything because everything was at stake. The Presidents. The Prime Ministers. The former Prime Ministers.

She thought of America and the despot, of Russia, and Ukraine, of Israel, and Palestine; of Yemen, and of Sudan; of body doubles, fake news, and the huge weight and interconnectedness and immediacy of ongoing aggression and catastrophes. A thought randomly dropped into her mind, of Castor and Pollux, the two elephants who had been eaten during the siege of Paris.

She woke each morning thinking, where were the ones she loved? They were there and not there. She did not have a way to make it all make sense.

Everything was

impossible. How could loss of so much be so simultaneous, she would have asked if, just then, she had been able to put the feeling into words.

Meaning exploded with each bomb.

Sometimes, the dead wandered into the house, congenially threw themselves down in a chair with all the force of habit and expectation she had come to know when they were alive. Sometimes the elsewhere dead came, too, from their cars or unsafe houses, riddled with bullets, or with breath shaken from them, flames in their clothes or hair.

Harms forced themselves on her and transformed into errant neurochemicals so that she woke from sleep, her heart pounding. Body parts exploded around her and children gathered them in terrible open-netted bags.

Her daughter had been sanguine and efficient as she straightened bedsheets and pillows, as once she had straightened her own dead husband's.

The virus, the smallest, mutest thing she could imagine, had crept into her, bedded itself in her lungs, swum and struggled to keep itself alive in her blood vessels, and all four chambers of her heart. Not

from love, but from desire, desire to be alive and to keep her alive, however painfully, in the process. As if, she said to herself, as if a virus even had agency beyond the structures of its own activity. Intelligence. The speed of light.

Though her heart, she knew, had been broken

had broken with a dull internal thud like

the soft sound of an apple suddenly released from a tree. Who, then, but the virus, could have felt that, inhabiting it, and her, cell by cell?

Sometimes

she wondered if what she wanted was to avoid being human at all —

to return to a place without language where she was all sound and fur and
gesture and breath.   But all the little breakages of words

now meant nothing,

and assembling it all was a question of how it could all possibly hold.

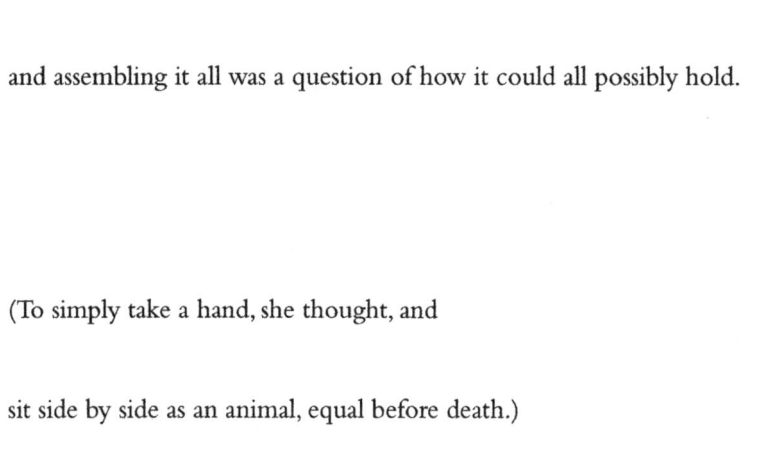

(To simply take a hand, she thought, and

sit side by side as an animal, equal before death.)

And, in spite of his death, all those years ago, it was her husband who visited most. He watched her while she slept. He criticised her cooking. He advised her, still, on the organisation of books, children, lives. Sometimes it felt as if he ran through her like time itself, a watermark, unmovable and translucent. He silently weighed up the character traits of other, newer lovers, nodded and sang and tightened his lips. Often, she'd smile and nod back at him or tell him gently to buzz off. Did he not have anything better to do with his time, she'd whisper, as he left her plane tickets on open webpages, placed unused train tickets or scribbled comments inside her favourite books.

But now he watched as she sweated, as the virus slowly took possession of her, and he moved with her between the worlds of the living and the dead. *Mon amour.*

People cooking, acting, dancing, sleeping, people making love,   and
singing. ~~Mothers no strike that out now~~, Parents looking after children,
cleaning noses, nappies, washing away the dirt, soothing the urine-burnt
skin. Parents pushing the hair from the foreheads of their offspring,
mopping up the vomit, milk, blue milk, the wet, hot brows. Joy. The tiny
frond-like movements of a baby's fingers. Parents weeping over bodies.
Donkey carts over poor roads.
The unburied dead.

— I would like to think that I have held things together
— When he held me
— When my son and daughter took my hand as we walked for the first
   time to the cemetery
— The first thing that comes to mind when holding a dead child is
   holding

                              your own child, someone said

And as she watched death at 24x a second on a movie screen

[pause]

[There's a memory I have, both fucked up & beautiful, of you
dead, and me beside you. I was like a dog who'd never slept,
guarding its owner, till the credits rolled. I was not quite sure what to
do with the gone-ness of you. When the nurses came, untethered you
like a vessel, from the sub-cut pump, they looked around, took
the morphine phials and broke them, crushing the glass like
dancers in slo-mo: flamenco, tender, in their neat black shoes. And

what I remember was being alone, and holding your hand, not
knowing that this peace, love, end of love and all its stuff would
lodge inside me like that broken glass, the slow procession as you
left the house, and me with your wedding ring that someone had
pulled off. I'd keep it at a distance, all this, like a lion tamer
in a small room and those nurses stamping. I don't think I'm exaggerating
when I say that each time that I lay down it would feel too much.]

*Some people lose control of their bladder and bowel as they
approach the end of life. This is normal but can be
embarrassing for you and those around you*

*It may feel strange to need so much help, but this can be a very
intimate and special time*

When you are awake and can talk, and then ease back into

*The final moments of life are usually very peaceful. Your
breathing may gradually become even slower   with very
long pauses   between each breath*

From her window in Paris (though still she did not know this yet) she could see the remains of Notre-Dame after the fire.

If you looked from the front,

it was as if
the cathedral was unharmed.

But from here,

on the right bank, looking up towards her, framed on an axis between the Eiffel Tower and the Panthéon, she sat under the wires and poles and steel and netting like a
wounded bird. Cordistes from all over the country had

been brought in after the fire like a small army of spiders – to hook and swing and secure the carcass – so that a web of ropes and wires held her together. Work continued in the day and in the night. The flames had gutted her innards and now robots were programmed to clear out the debris, which was painstakingly photographed, piece by broken piece. What was being restored? Or recovered? Or found. And what would be left

behind? Her daughter enlarged small maps and images to show her the heads of former kings unearthed, their heads sliced from the stone and buried along with the recently living.

Beside her, the Hôtel de Dieu was also under
renovation, and, if you peered through the modern glass

you could see, like an hallucination, or a fall back into time, the cool stones of the old hospital.

(On the coast, in the Children's Hotels, the rooms were emptying.

I dreamt about them, someone said. I could see their

hands and stars streaming in their black hair as they closed doors behind them, as they were rushed away.)

There were mosquito warnings in the city.

The feverish planet meant that the insects had travelled north with their viruses. Zika. Dengue.

She dreamt about her daughter, a teen bride in an orange Biba dress. And when she woke, the room felt less safe than

before. An insect had left huge red welts on her arms and face.

In the Jardin des Plantes they had built a technicolour forest of enormous plastic insects and flowers. Grasshoppers. Maybugs. Bullrushes. Yellow and purple flowers. She stepped slowly around them as if in some slo-mo slalem

and then stopped to rest in the café at the nearby mosque. She watched the sparrows thread in and out of the vines.

Later, she took a photograph of herself

in an exhibition where everything distorted
and refracted into mirrors like a world

riddled with gunshot.

She wrote letters and waited for letters. For a week the internet connection was down and each day, several times a day, she would sit in the park to establish a connection on the city's open wifi. She would speak to her providers. Samson and Sylvienne, who took her calls, spoke with exaggerated politeness and asked her to be patient, as if she were a small child.

(To love, to be comforted.
To love, to be conflicted.)

And so the future sat, waiting for her like —

like she did not know quite what.

Now the joiner had begun to whistle and, from the garden, where she was now sitting, she could hear the tap of a hammer, the sound of something being made to open and close.

In her phone, an invitation popped up to attend a discussion about desire with artists and philosophers. It was accompanied by a Renaissance depiction of Adam and Eve in the garden by the artist Lucas Cranach.

Tangles of vines were placed over their genitalia and seemed so much a

part of their bodies that in fact they became their genitals. Leafy pubis erased phalluses and transformed into vegetation and around them animals paused reminding us

no doubt of the deer-like qualities of Eve, the dog eyes of Adam. Eve's hair rippled and rustled with the leaves. The garden: not left, but reinvented, in the now of the frame.

She thought of another painting, 'Cupid Complaining to Venus', the little boy holding the honeycomb, his flesh stung by bees.

And then became distracted.

Her own dog, named for spring, was sitting now, companionably, at her feet, occasionally making noises to remind her of something, of the future, of the wildness of the garden, of the joiner, of everything now that was being brought together.

Soon the joiner would summon her back upstairs to inspect the window.

Did she want to check the mechanism?

He could show her how smoothly it ran on its tracks again and warn her to be more gentle.

Up would go the window and down would go the window, like the before and after, like a guillotine.

At some point

in the future

she would open the window

and lean out one early evening

and look out at the overgrown garden, and something in her would

settle

even as the blue beyond that deepened and deepens into

night, settled, fractured and realigned. Even — and she saw now her hand
her trembling —

as the damaged world shivered and tilted on its axis.

And she went over the names of plants and flowers in another language,
watching their shape and textures flare and flame and change as she spoke
them.

(At which point in her thinking, the joiner left, his bag on his shoulder,
leaving a bill in her outstretched palm.)

Later, much later, she would look down at her phone to messages from her son who was staying in a hostel

near to the old hotel. It would be Easter.

From somewhere came the thread of sound.

Pink blossom. Riots. Fires.

When she called out was there really nothing?

From the hurt skies and broken roots and branches the sound made itself over and over and hummed and settled as if there were some dome or great bell into which all things were drawn and resonated. The cells and the smaller than cells, the plants and the animals, rose up and translated themselves and there it was again, beauty and fragile things that found for a while a voice and a tempo and a pitch to answer her call, become her call, make of her a call and its listening, dipping in and out of time, with an ungovernable sweetness. . . .

The world would pour out its tragedies and dissonances and repetitions. They were at war. She would step into the world. She would listen; she would call out; she would do what she could. She would think of her own heart, sitting snug beside her left lung, and the steady if uneven frame each lung-wing made inside her.

She would sink down and let her body hold her in a gesture of relief and weight and lightness and pain. She would hold her children close. She would think of the lighthouse, of bees, and drones,

and all the unspoken and untranslatable spaces; she would think of the lost languages; and she would tend her small garden. The great breathing tree that was no longer there would hang, nevertheless, like a ghost in the air.

She would lie down at night with her ear pressed to her lover's chest, and she would take in the slow steady steps of his heart, feel his breath on her cheek,

as if listening to a distant ocean; she would let its slow pull bring her to and from the shore.

She would watch as cornflowers, poppies, stock, rose

from his belly and ribs, as if from bombed ruins,

and look up as they fired themselves & flamed from scars on his hands, his ribs, from the soft creases behind his knees.

The woman at the airport had asked her to hold out her arms

which she did.

She felt like a tree,

an easel, an angel.

She closed her eyes as the woman, with her blue-gloved hands, ran a machine up and down her arms, in the v between her breasts, around her thighs and waist.

The woman held the machine like a wand, and it bleeped as she followed the lines of her body, drew out her shape like a child drawing the figure of a human.

Into what

might she transform?

As it caught hold of buttons and wires, and keys, the wand bleeped again
and she emptied out her pockets.

Years seeped into and through her. She imagined herself, the wrinkles
round her eyes like bark, or the desiccated skin of an elephant.

Beside her, passengers were occupied in the act
of taking off their coats and shoes and placing their belongings in the
plastic trays for the X-ray machines.

Her arms raised, she looked up, and slightly ahead,
posed in a state
of momentary surrender.

And then, like a wing-flap in slow motion, she slowly let her hands fall
again at her side.

With a nod, the woman at security
waved her through.

She would walk, hesitantly at first,
her luggage collected from the

carousel. And then,
with something

that felt like a new rhythm,
she would pick up speed,

look up, head out
towards the departures gate

—When I woke there was an emergency
We stood listening to the sirens and your whole face

pulsed
and we were still, so still

—When I woke there was sunlight, small patches of light pushing through
the faded bedroom curtains. My body rested there on cotton sheets.

—When I woke the room was bare, windowless and my body
broke open — dust motes — cells

I had almost disappeared

—When I woke, I looked up at the ceiling and watched light slowly enter
in —

We were too scared to be afraid.

— It was a revelation. The small room papered in repeating rosebud
patterns, (the small room, empty, dirty), the strip of lawn outside, the
pigeons and their sounds like wood blown up against my mouth, the wind

— I had stepped into another time. A small flower quivered on a ledge.
A bird sang from the meadow.

~~little~~
~~sharp-beaked, brown bird, throat open,~~
~~wise bird, jazz riff, cello start, sad techno,~~
~~harder heart, self-broken / broken part, half~~
~~noun, verb start, bird till-death=~~
~~and=dearest=part, quickening and~~
~~shard part, splintering and feather voice,~~
~~box lung, thrust voice, high strutter, sky grazer,~~
~~floor grazer, leaf layer, gallant player, lust sung,~~
~~here we are alone together.~~

Departure. Delay.

Someone was speaking, and from somewhere a voice found itself and
lifted itself into song

And I brought with me this,
which my grandmother had given me,
a tiny elephant on a string.

Acknowledgements

Thanks to the Cité Internationale des Arts, Paris, for the residency in 2022; also, to *Neue Vocalsolisten*, Stuttgart, especially Christine and Andreas Fischer; and my collaborator, Bnaya Halperin-Kaddari, whose artistic companionship on this journey towards recovery has been such a pleasure.

Deep gratitude to early readers, especially Colette Bryce, Anthony Rudolf, Eira Murphy, Sasha Dugdale, Jonathan Ellis, Maurice Riordan, Sandeep Parmar, George Szirtes; and to Alison Mark, Judith Palmer, Catherine Marcangeli, Samera Naji, and Maky Amanuel who kept me going at the best and worst of times. Thanks to my editors Zoë Brigley and Rhian Edwards, and all the team at Seren; at the University of Liverpool, to my colleagues and students. Particular thanks, too, to Ben Lloyd; and to Dr Justine Hadcroft, poetry lover in the Department of Respiratory Medicine.

Quotes from *A Midsummer Night's Dream* are taken from the translation by Victor Hugo. Sonnet (ii) quotes from a letter from Tsvetayeva to Rilke in which she quotes Rilke's own lines back at him, in *Letters Summer 1926: Correspondence Between Boris Pasternak, Marina Tsvetayeva and Rainer Maria Rilke*, edited by Yevgeny Pasternak and Konstantin M Azadovsky; translated by Margaret Wettlin and Walter Arndt (Oxford: Oxford University Press, 1988); sonnet (vi) references Spenser's sonnet 71. Sonnet (xiv) quotes from Shakespeare's sonnet 40. Sonnet (xix) begins with a quote from Paul Celan, from his lecture 'The Meridian' (1960). The passage continues: 'It is lonely and en route. Its author stays with it. Does this very fact not place the poem already here, at its inception, in the encounter, *in the mystery of encounter?*'. I am grateful to Sasha Dugdale for sharing with me her new unpublished translation of Tsvetayeva's 'Poem of the Air', written to Rilke after his death, from which sonnet (xx) quotes. Sonnet (xxii) quotes from John Donne's 'A Nocturnal upon St Lucy's Day'. Sonnet (xxiv) quotes from Wordsworth's 'Tintern Abbey'. Lines about end-of-life care are taken, near verbatim, from Macmillan's *A Guide to the End of Life*. I am grateful for John Hersey's book *Hiroshima* (1985).

Elsewhere, lines and references to pictures and from films and songs inevitably drift in.

Thanks to the editors of *Poetry Ireland Review, Odes to John Keats* (2019), *The Guardian*, and *Poetry London*, where some of these poems, in various versions, first appeared.

This book is in memory of my beloved parents-in-law Terry Murphy (1931-2023) and Gladys Murphy (1938-2024); and it is for Eira and Felix: for their late nights and early mornings; for all their conversations, their brilliance, and care, and love.